DISNEY's
THE NEW ADVENTURES OF
WINNIE the POOH
Caws and Effect

TWIN BOOKS

MALLARD PRESS

To Rabbit, harvest time was the most wonderful time of the year. He bustled about collecting his gardening supplies and piling them into the arms of Winnie the Pooh.

"May I help you harvest your garden?" asked Pooh.

Rabbit was so excited, he was shaking. "Oh, no, Pooh Bear! I could never trust anyone else with that. Why, I hardly trust myself!"

2

3

Rabbit's mouth dropped open when he glanced at his lovely garden. "Crows!" he screamed. "Quickly, Pooh Bear, hand me my broom!

"Trespassers!" Rabbit shouted as he rushed at the terrified crows. "I'll make feather dusters of you all!"

Pooh reached into his armful of gardening supplies and pulled out a feather duster.

"No, no, Pooh! The broom!" screamed Rabbit. "Aaaagh! If there's one thing I hate more than a crow, it's four crows!"

Rabbit chased off the crows, but he realized he would need help if they came back. It was time to call in the troops!

Later that morning, Rabbit paraded past his recruits, Tigger and Piglet. He pointed to a makeshift curtain. "The purpose of this drill," said Rabbit in his best military-type voice, "is to make you familiar with the filthiest, trickiest, most evil enemy the gardener has ever faced!"

"Oh, d-dear!" said Piglet.

Rabbit tore back the curtain. "The crow!" announced Rabbit, indicating a strange character in costume. "Notice how his beady little eyes are just looking for the chance to rob my garden!"

"That's odd," said Tigger. "It looks like Pooh."

Pooh leaned forward to Tigger, winked and whispered, "Don't tell anyone, but actually...I'm me."

"Pooh Bear!" said Rabbit, frowning.

"Sorry, Rabbit," said Pooh. He raised his beak, flapped his wings and said, "Caw! Ahem...caw!"

"Oh, d-dear!" said Piglet for the second time.

"Don't be afraid, Piglet," said Rabbit. "By pretending that Pooh is a crow, we're just going to practice stopping others like him from stealing. Aren't we, Pooh?"

"Caw," said Pooh.

"This'll do if there's just one crow," Tigger pointed out, "but what if there's a gazillion of them?"

Rabbit turned around, reached into a wheelbarrow, and pulled out four dummies stuffed with straw.

"The crows will see these, think we've doubled our number, and run for their lives!" he explained proudly.

Rabbit picked up a butterfly net. "Watch very closely," he instructed. "Do just as I do!"

Pooh flapped his wings and ran around in circles. Rabbit tried to catch Pooh with his net and missed. He missed again, and yet again. His net hit the ground—*fwap, fwap, fwap!*

Tigger and Piglet began to slap their nets to the ground—*fwap, fwap, fwap!*

"No, no, no!" screamed Rabbit.

Rabbit kicked the ground in anger. His foot hit a rock and he cried out. "Ow! Oohoo!" He hopped up and down on one foot.

Tigger and Piglet looked at each other, shrugged, and started hopping up and down on one foot. "Ow! Oohoo!" they cried.

Rabbit had had enough. "Stop that! Stop that this instant!" He put his whistle to his lips.

The sound of the whistle caught everyone's attention, especially Rabbit's. He was puzzled because he hadn't blown his whistle yet.

It was one of the crows that had whistled. He whistled again, just to make certain that everyone saw him. Then he flew into the garden, grabbed a big, juicy tomato, and escaped into the woods.

"A crow!" screamed Rabbit. "Pooh Bear, stay here and guard my garden until help arrives!"

"Caw, caw," said Pooh. "Where are you going?"

"After that crow!" shouted Rabbit, and he charged into the woods. Tigger and Piglet raised their nets and charged after Rabbit.

The crow left a trail that even Tigger couldn't miss. Feathers were scattered all over the ground.

Tigger turned to Rabbit and said, "We're either following a crow or a leaky pillow!"

Rabbit glanced back the way they had come. "I do hope Pooh is taking good care of my garden," he fretted.

Piglet smiled. "Don't worry, Rabbit," he said. "I'm sure everything will be just fine!" Then, with a worried frown, he whispered to himself, "I hope."

Piglet was right to be concerned. At that very moment, the other crows were in Rabbit's garden, painting themselves red to look like tomatoes.

"Hacawcaw, hacawcaw!" snickered one of the crows.

"Shhhh!" warned another crow.

Pooh heard the sounds, turned from his guard post, and saw some leaves rustling in the garden. "I wonder if that's the plants calling out to be harvested," he said.

Pooh walked over to the garden and saw the three painted crows. "Why, hello," he said. "Who are you?" But, since tomatoes don't talk, the crows said nothing.

"Let me guess," said Pooh. "Are you tomatoes?" The crows smiled and nodded their heads.

"I never knew tomatoes could nod their heads," said Pooh, puzzled.

The crows smiled even wider and nodded again.

"Oh, good," said Pooh. "For a moment, I thought you might be crows." The crows frowned and shook their heads.

"I know!" said Pooh. "You must be the help that Rabbit said would arrive!" Again, the crows nodded.

"How do you do? I'm Pooh," said Pooh. "Have you flown in from the North?" The crows continued to nod.

"But you couldn't be penguins. You're a much warmer color," said Pooh. "Perhaps you are from the South?"

The crows nodded again, eagerly, and piled vegetables on top of their heads. Then they began to dance, as if they were from a sunny land down south.

Pooh watched the crows dance through the garden. It looked like so much fun that he decided to join them.

The crows picked and juggled the vegetables, then passed them back to Pooh so they could pick and juggle some more. In no time, Pooh found his arms full of vegetables. He hadn't thought harvesting would be so much fun.

Meanwhile, Piglet looked around the woods and said, "Oh, dear! I wonder where we are."

"That's easy," said Tigger, pointing to the ground. "We're right here!"

"And where is right here?" asked Rabbit.

Tigger waved his arm and said, "Just a little northwest of that tree over there. See? Tiggers never get lost!"

"I hope not," said Rabbit. "And I hope my garden's all right."

The fourth crow donned a red, tomatoey-looking cape and got back to Rabbit's house just as the harvest feast was about to begin. He was welcomed by his friends with open wings and pats on the back for a job well done.

Pooh set a large plate of food on Rabbit's table. He saw the new arrival and said, "Oh, another guest! Is this going to be a feast for friends?"

The four crows smiled at Pooh and nodded their heads.

The crows sat down at the table, licking their beaks.

Pooh said, "If this is a feast for friends, perhaps I should get Rabbit, Tigger, and Piglet to join us!"

At the mention of Rabbit's name, the crows leaped back from the table and shook their heads wildly. Pooh was confused.

"But don't you want them to see what a fine job we've done with the harvest?" said Pooh.

The crows shook their heads even harder.

"I know!" said Pooh, brightening. "I've just thought of a wonderful way they can be here...sort of."

Rabbit, Tigger, and Piglet had gone as far as they could.

"We've walked a very great distance and found very few crows," said Piglet.

Rabbit nodded. "Yes," he said. "This was nothing but a wild goose chase!"

"Goose?" said Tigger. "I thought we were looking for crows!"

Rabbit sighed as he turned to lead the way home.

The crows didn't know where Pooh had gone. They didn't care. They just sat back down at the table. But before any of them could take a bite, there was a knock at the door.

Turning to watch the door swing open, the crows gasped in fear. In the doorway stood a smiling Pooh with the dummies of Rabbit, Tigger, and Piglet behind him.

Of course, the crows didn't know that the dummies weren't the real Rabbit, Tigger, and Piglet.

"Surprise!" cried Pooh.

Pooh had never seen anyone move so fast. The crows got stuck in the window in their rush to get out of the house.

"Where are you going in such a hurry?" asked Pooh.

The crows didn't stop to answer. They bumped and shoved each other until they were finally out the window.

"I wonder why they didn't use the door," said Pooh.

"Crows!" screamed Rabbit as he approached his house with Tigger and Piglet.

"I didn't know crows changed color in autumn," said Tigger.

"Oh, Rabbit!" said Piglet. "Look at your garden!"

"It's ruined!" said Rabbit. "Destroyed! Oh, why did I ever trust that fumbling, bumbling bear to guard it?"

Rabbit stalked angrily toward his house.

"Pooh Bear!" shouted Rabbit as he entered his house. "I can't believe that you…you…" He stared in shock at the feast spread out on his table.

"Why, Pooh," said Rabbit, "you harvested my garden!"

"How did you do it, Buddy Bear?" asked Tigger.

"It was easy," said Pooh as he danced around the room. "A carrot here, a turnip there, and a little help from my friends."

Rabbit, Tigger, and Piglet looked at each other. Which friends was Pooh talking about?

All the adventures of the day were soon forgotten, as Rabbit, Tigger, and Piglet joined Pooh in his dance around the harvest table.

Everyone had a wonderful time, especially Rabbit. It was his most wonderful day of the year.